Merida
Legend of the Emeralds

By Ellie O'Ryan
Illustrated by
the Disney Storybook Artists

DISNEP PRESS
New York • Los Angeles

ABDO
Spotlight

ABDOPUBLISHING.COM

Reinforced library bound edition published in 2018 by Spotlight, a division of ABDO, PO Box 398166, Minneapolis, Minnesota 55439. Spotlight produces high-quality reinforced library bound editions for schools and libraries. Published by agreement with Disney Press.

Printed in the United States of America, North Mankato, Minnesota.
092017
012018

THIS BOOK CONTAINS
RECYCLED MATERIALS

LIBRARY OF CONGRESS CATALOGING-IN-PUBLICATION DATA

This book was previously cataloged with the following information:

O'Ryan, Ellie.
   Merida : legend of the emeralds / by Ellie O'Ryan ; illustrated by the Disney Storybook Artists.
      p. cm. (Disney Princess)
Summary: During the Rites of Summer games, Merida and Young Macintosh discover two glowing emeralds that hold the secret to an ancient legend.
   1. Emeralds--Juvenile fiction. 2. Legends--Juvenile fiction. 3. Princesses--Juvenile fiction. 4. Adventure stories. 5. Emeralds--Fiction. 6. Legends--Fiction. 7. Princesses--Fiction. 8. Adventure and adventurers--Fiction.
PZ7.O78417 Mc 2014
[Fic]--dc23
                              2012954511

978-1-5321-4121-8   (Reinforced Library Bound Edition)

Spotlight
A Division of ABDO
abdopublishing.com

CHAPTER ONE

Princess Merida raced down the hallway as fast as she could. Her feet clattered across the stone floor of the castle. As she dashed around a corner, Merida nearly crashed right into Maudie, one of the servants.

Maudie gasped in surprise, steadying the tray of desserts she was carrying. She had jumped out of the way just in time.

"Sorry!" Merida called as she adjusted the

quiver full of arrows slung over her shoulder. She knew that her mother, Queen Elinor, wouldn't approve of her running in the castle, but Merida just couldn't slow down. She was too excited!

Throughout the long, dark winter and the damp spring, Merida had looked forward to the Rites of Summer. The special festival celebrated summertime and the strong friendship between the clans. It had been decided months ago that the Macintosh clan would be the DunBroch clan's honored guests this year. Upon the arrival of the Macintoshes, the two clans would celebrate together with a day of dancing, games, and feats of strength. The Rites of Summer was one of Merida's favorite celebrations.

Merida's long red curls bounced wildly as she burst into the Great Hall. The biggest room in the castle was more crowded than usual. Queen Elinor was supervising the servants as they finished getting ready for the festival. In the middle of all the commotion, Merida's father, King Fergus, wrestled with her triplet brothers, Harris, Hubert, and Hamish.

Queen Elinor looked up from a scroll of parchment paper. "A princess never runs in the castle," she reminded Merida.

"But Mum!" Merida exclaimed. "It's the Rites of Summer!"

"Even so, a princess must always behave with the proper dignity," Queen Elinor gently replied.

"You were just warming up for the races this afternoon, weren't you, lass?" King Fergus asked Merida with a wink. "I'm sure on an *ordinary* day, you'd never be running through the castle like a shrieking banshee, would you?"

Merida and her father started laughing.

Even Queen Elinor had to smile. It wasn't so long ago that Merida and her mum disagreed about almost everything. Queen Elinor believed that a princess should be ladylike at all times. She wanted Merida to be prepared for when she would one day be a queen herself. Elinor had even arranged a competition so that suitors from the nearby clans could compete to marry Merida.

But Merida didn't like having her life planned out for her. She wanted to race on her horse, Angus, and practice her archery. More than anything, Merida wanted to choose her own fate. She and Elinor hadn't started to understand each other until they were forced to work together. Since then, Merida and her mum had tried hard to get along better. It wasn't always easy, but they were both determined to do their best.

Today, Queen Elinor's focus on the proper behavior gave Merida an idea.

"Please, Mum," Merida said, "isn't it time to start the processional? If we leave now, we could reach the dock in time to welcome the Macintosh clan. We might even be able to see the ships arrive!"

Queen Elinor looked thoughtful. "It seems a wee bit early," she replied. "Let me check the schedule."

While Queen Elinor consulted her scroll, Merida reached for a charm that dangled from her bow. It was made of smooth stone that had been carved into the shape of a thistle. Whenever Merida thought she might need a little luck, she always rubbed one of her charms. The thistle was her favorite.

"Usually, the processional starts at half past nine," Queen Elinor continued. "Then everyone returns to the castle by eleven to set up the visitors' tents. King Fergus and I issue the formal welcome to the Rites by one o'clock, during the afternoon feast. After that, the games and contests last until six, the evening feast begins at seven, and the music and dancing will continue until the first light of morning."

Merida held her breath as she waited for her mother to make a decision. The thistle charm grew warm from the heat of Merida's hand.

"But I see no reason why we shouldn't

begin the processional a little earlier than usual this year," Queen Elinor finally decided. "The ships are always a sight to behold!"

Before Queen Elinor could say another word, Merida was on her way outside.

"Merida, wait!" the queen called after her.

Reluctantly, Merida paused just inside the heavy oak door.

"First your father, then I, *then* you, and then the triplets," Queen Elinor said firmly.

Merida grinned sheepishly as her family took their positions. Then they stepped into the dazzling sunshine as other members of the DunBroch clan fell into place behind them. Bagpipers played merry songs as girls from the village tossed rose petals into the air. The processional wove its way through

brilliant green hillsides, past wild thistles and the first roses of summer. Merida could smell the ocean as they approached the dock. Though the sun was shining brightly, a silvery mist hung over the water. Suddenly, the mist cleared. There, in the distance, Merida saw it: the Macintosh clan's lead ship!

Merida jumped up and down with excitement.

The Rites of Summer was about to begin!

CHAPTER TWO

$\mathscr{A}$s the Macintosh clan rowed up to the dock, Merida could hear the clansmen singing a rousing song of summer. They were just as excited about the festival as the DunBroch clan was.

"Oi! DunBroch!" a voice bellowed from the deck of the boat. It was Lord Macintosh.

"Oi! Macintosh!" King Fergus roared back.

"To the Rites!" both rulers yelled together. The DunBroch and Macintosh clans burst into cheers.

"Oi! Merida!" a new voice called out.

Merida looked up to see Young Macintosh climbing off the boat. Merida hadn't seen Young Macintosh since the competition for her hand in marriage, but his confident swagger hadn't changed a bit.

Merida watched Young Macintosh run up to her. He was tall and athletic, with a swirl of blue paint on his right arm. Merida wondered if he'd ever start painting blue streaks on his face, like his father, Lord Macintosh, did.

"Oi! Young Macintosh!" Merida replied. "I see you've come to impress us with your feats of strength again."

"And impressed you'll be, I'm sure," he said, puffing out his chest proudly. The sunlight glinted off a ring of silver that was fastened to his kilt sash.

"What's that, now?" Merida asked curiously.

Young Macintosh polished the ring with his hand. "It's the Macintosh crest," he told her.

"Oh, fancy, are we?" Merida teased. But she knew that Young Macintosh had every reason to be pleased with his crest. A family crest was very special.

"Don't you have a crest of your own?" Young Macintosh asked with a maddening grin.

"No—but I have these," Merida replied, showing him the charms on her bow.

"What is that, a thistle?" Young Macintosh said as he glanced at one of the charms. "That's fitting for you. You're both prickly and stubborn."

"I'd rather be prickly like a thistle than arrogant like a peacock!" Merida snapped.

"Who are you calling a peacock?" Young Macintosh demanded.

Merida opened her eyes wide. "Oh, nobody," she said, shifting her bow from one arm to the other. "A peacock surely couldn't shoot an arrow and make a bull's-eye three times in a row. What do you think—could *you?*"

"Of course I could," Young Macintosh announced, tossing his shiny black hair.

"Good!" Merida said brightly. "Let's go see

you do it, then. That's a fitting challenge to start the Rites of Summer." With that, Merida glanced over her shoulder. Her parents and Lord Macintosh had finished greeting each other and had begun leading the processional back toward the castle. She turned and ran up to her parents to join them.

"Wait!" Young Macintosh spoke up, approaching Merida. She could tell from the worried look on his face that he had remembered the last archery competition for Merida's hand in marriage. Not only had Young Macintosh's arrow missed the mark, he'd been so upset that he'd thrown a huge tantrum! Then Young Macintosh had banged his bow on the ground—and even thrown it into the crowd!

"Let's toss some cabers, instead," continued Young Macintosh. "Unless you don't think you can handle one."

Merida frowned. If she agreed to Young Macintosh's challenge, she'd be at a big disadvantage. The heavy cabers were made from tree trunks. Young Macintosh, with his large muscles, would almost certainly be able to throw one farther than Merida. She wanted to find a challenge where they would be evenly matched.

Soon, everyone had entered the castle and was buzzing with excitement about what the day had in store. Merida and Young Macintosh were lingering outside of

King Fergus's stables. With Queen Elinor supervising all the activity, Merida knew she and Young Macintosh wouldn't be missed. They just had to make it back to the castle in time for the welcoming ceremony and afternoon feast.

"How about a race, then?" Merida suggested. "A race . . . to the top . . . of the Fire Falls!"

Young Macintosh looked surprised. "To the top of the Fire Falls!" he exclaimed. "You could never make it!"

"Aye, I can. I have before," Merida replied confidently. "But if you're not certain you could make the climb, we can do something else."

"I'm an excellent climber—the best in

my clan!" Young Macintosh bragged.

"Then I'll be waiting for you at the top of the falls—after I win!" cried Merida. She looped her bow over her shoulder, headed over to her horse, Angus, and raced away from the castle.

Young Macintosh recognized a challenge when he saw one. With a loud whoop, he ducked into the king's stables, climbed onto one of the horses, and took off after Merida.

"You can't possibly think you'll make it to the top before I do!" Young Macintosh called.

"Oh, I don't think it," Merida said. "I know it!"

Angus galloped forward with an extra burst of speed, but Young Macintosh's horse was already right beside him. They

raced through fields where purple-headed thistles poked up from soft green grass. Then Merida thought of a shortcut. She steered Angus into a forest of ancient trees, with Young Macintosh and his steed just steps away. The dim forest was full of shadows, but the horses were sure-footed as they stepped over twisted roots. Merida and Young Macintosh reached the Fire Falls at the same time, tethered the horses, and began to climb the craggy rocks.

"You might as well stay at the bottom," Young Macintosh yelled over the rushing of the waterfall. "I'll reach the top and be back down again before you've even gone halfway!"

"Don't be a numpty!" Merida retorted. "I've done this climb more times than you.

I've even drunk from the Fire Falls, just like the ancient kings."

"I'll believe that when I see it." Young Macintosh laughed.

At that moment, Merida reached the Crone's Tooth, a rocky platform more than halfway up to the top. After making sure that Young Macintosh was watching, she leaned backward to take a big gulp of the sparkling water rushing over the falls. Despite himself, Young Macintosh looked impressed.

But in a flash, he took advantage of Merida's pause and climbed into the lead!

"See you at the top!" he called.

Merida gritted her teeth and raced to catch up. Soon, she and Young Macintosh were neck and neck.

At the very top of the falls, Merida used a last burst of strength to pull herself over the rocky ledge. "I won! I did it," she gasped.

"You did no such thing!" argued Young Macintosh. He had also reached the top.

"Aye, I did," she shot back. "My hand was over the rock first."

"But my hand is bigger than yours," Young Macintosh snapped. "So it was farther over the rock, which means I won."

Merida put her hands on her hips. "I think your head is dizzy from the climb—" she started to say.

Then Merida stopped herself. She knew that her mum wouldn't want her to insult one of their guests during the Rites of Summer— even if he did deserve it. Instead, she knelt down by the stream to splash some cool water on her face. Young Macintosh did the same.

"This is a fine waterfall you've got here," Young Macintosh said in a friendlier tone. "I would climb these rocks all the time if I lived in DunBroch."

Merida wondered if he was trying to be on his best behavior, too. "I'm sure you would," she replied as she gazed out over the falls. She

could see some of the Macintosh clan's tents had already been set up. Merida knew that she and Young Macintosh had time before they were expected back at the castle—but not much.

Then Merida turned around. The flowing stream that fed the waterfall twisted through the landscape. Merida had watched the rushing Fire Falls since she was a young girl. But she had never given much thought as to where the water started.

"Where do you think the water comes from?" she asked Young Macintosh.

"You mean to say you don't know?" he said in surprise.

"No, I don't," Merida replied. "But today's the day I find out!"

CHAPTER THREE

"Oi, Merida, wait!" Young Macintosh called as he scrambled up to follow her. "Where are you going?"

"I just told you," Merida replied. "I'm going to find the source of the Fire Falls."

"But . . . today? Now?" Young Macintosh said doubtfully. He glanced back toward the castle. "Shouldn't we go back for the Rites? Your mum—"

"If you're 'feert, go back to DunBroch," Merida teased. "I'm sure you can manage to find your way."

"I've never been 'feert in my life," Young Macintosh bragged, puffing out his chest. "Even as a wee baby!"

"Oh, really?" Merida teased him. "Because I noticed that you didn't drink from the Fire Falls during our climb, and I couldn't figure out why. Of course, most people would be 'feert to lean backwards from such a height—"

"I wasn't 'feert," Young Macintosh scoffed.

Merida and Young Macintosh kept bickering as they walked along the twisting stream. The shrubs grew thicker, full of brambles and wild berries. Merida stepped carefully to avoid the thorns. Soon, the bushes were so dense that it was difficult to see anything but dark green leaves all around her. Her heart started pounding in her chest as she pushed the branches aside. She knew that they were near the source of the Fire Falls.

Then Merida stopped short. She found herself standing at the edge of an ordinary-looking loch. Not a bird chirped; not a beetle buzzed. There was a strange stillness around the loch, as if it hadn't been disturbed for ages.

Young Macintosh's voice shattered the silence. "Not much to see here," he announced. "Just a regular loch, isn't it?" Young Macintosh picked up a pebble and threw it from the shore. The stone skimmed across the water, leaving rippling circles behind it. The ripples vanished almost as quickly as they had appeared.

Merida stared at the water in silence.

"Is something wrong?" Young Macintosh finally asked her.

"I thought it would be something more," Merida replied. "I fancied we would have an adventure, but the source of the Fire Falls is nothing more than . . . a common loch, isn't it?"

Merida leaned down to skim her fingers through the loch. The water was surprisingly cool, even though the day had grown quite warm.

When she stood up again, Merida

leaned against a boulder that was covered with flowering vines. She turned away so that Young Macintosh wouldn't see how disappointed she was. As she turned, her shoe caught on a root, causing her to lose her footing for a moment.

Suddenly, Merida cried out in surprise: the boulder had begun to move! As it shifted behind her, Merida stumbled backward and disappeared, swallowed up by a dark hole.

"Merida!" Young Macintosh yelled with concern. He charged toward the spot where Merida had been standing just moments ago. "Oi! Where are you?" he called into the darkness.

"I'm here," Merida's voice called out, with

a strange echo following it. "There's a cave behind the vines. And you'll never believe what I've found!"

"What's back there?" Young Macintosh asked.

"The *real* source of the Fire Falls," Merida replied. "That loch wasn't the source at all. Come see for yourself!"

Young Macintosh had no choice but to follow her. He stepped carefully into the cavern, holding on to the rocky wall with one hand for support. At first, it was very dark inside. If he strained his ears, he could hear a faint trickle of water.

Young Macintosh found Merida kneeling in the very center of the cave near a pool of water. Her hands were cupped around something that glowed. The golden light flickered over her face.

"Look at this," Merida whispered. "Have you ever, in all your life, seen anything like it?"

"What have you got there?" Young Macintosh asked, crouching next to Merida to get a better look. He saw a rough stone ledge in the middle of a shallow pool of water. Someone had carved a design along the edge of the stone. It looked like a chain of knots linked together by oval-shaped loops.

At that moment, Merida moved her hands, flooding the cave with a beautiful light. Young Macintosh blinked in surprise at two large, glowing emeralds sitting on the ledge in front of them.

"These emeralds—someone must have put them here," Merida said.

"Look at the water seeping onto the stone," Young Macintosh said. "It must come from underground."

"The water swirls around the emeralds and trickles off the ledge," Merida realized. "Then it flows down through the loch and becomes the Fire Falls!"

Merida cautiously reached out to touch the emeralds. "I've never seen emeralds glow like this. They must be very lucky."

"Lucky? Why's that?" asked Young Macintosh.

"Because emeralds bring good luck, of course," Merida replied. "Everyone knows that."

Young Macintosh started to laugh. "No, that's all wrong," he said confidently. "My father told me that emeralds are a symbol of power. In ancient times, lords paid tribute to great kings with emeralds. My father said that one king's vault had more than a thousand sparkling emeralds inside!"

Now it was Merida's turn to laugh. "A thousand emeralds? There can't be that many in all the land!" she exclaimed.

Young Macintosh glared at her. "I suppose you think you know more than my father, then—the great ruler of the Macintosh clan!"

"Your father is as mistaken as you are," Merida said firmly. "Emeralds have always been lucky for our people."

Then, to Merida's surprise, Young Macintosh grabbed one of the emeralds! He jammed it into the pouch attached to his kilt.

"Put that back!" Merida ordered.

"I'll do no such thing," he said. "Emeralds mean power, and I'm bringing this back for my father. The Macintosh clan will be stronger than ever!"

Merida's eyes flashed angrily. "Then I'll be

taking this one," she said as she plucked the other emerald from the ledge. She shoved it into the leather pouch on her belt. The emerald was so large that Merida couldn't completely close the pouch's drawstring around it. "And you can see for yourself the good luck it will bring to all of the people of DunBroch!"

Merida and Young Macintosh made their way out of the cave, arguing all the way back to DunBroch Castle.

With the emeralds hidden in their pouches, neither one noticed that the gems had stopped glowing.

CHAPTER FOUR

*M*erida arrived at the castle with Young Macintosh just in time for the welcoming ceremony and afternoon feast. Every single member of their clans was streaming into the Great Hall for the first official event of the Rites of Summer. The servants piled the tables high with the very best food in all of DunBroch.

Merida shook her head as she noticed her

little brothers gnawing on pheasant legs. No one was supposed to start eating until King Fergus and Queen Elinor had given a formal welcome to the visiting clan.

At the front of the hall, a long wooden table had been placed on a platform. It was reserved for Merida's and Young Macintosh's families. By eating together in front of their clansmen, the royal families set an example of friendship. From a distance, it looked like Queen Elinor was chatting happily with Lord Macintosh. But her eyes were worried as she glanced around the Great Hall from table to table. At last, she spotted Merida and breathed a sigh of relief.

"Merida, the welcoming ceremony is about to begin!" Queen Elinor exclaimed. "Where have you been?"

Young Macintosh started to snicker as if Merida were in trouble. "Mum, I have a question," Merida began, ignoring him. "What's the meaning of an emerald?"

"Ahh, lass, I can answer you that," Lord Macintosh broke in. "The emerald has long been a symbol of power and strength to every clan in our great land."

Young Macintosh's eyes lit up. "Just like I told you!" he jeered.

Lord Macintosh grabbed his son's chin, wiping the goofy grin right off the boy's face. "What've I told you about minding your manners?" he scolded. "You're not to be rude to our hosts on this day of celebration."

"Lord Macintosh is correct. Emeralds do symbolize power," Queen Elinor said.

"But they are also important gems to our people. In fact, the emerald carries a variety of significant meanings, wouldn't you agree, Lord Macintosh?"

Lord Macintosh looked a little flustered. "Well—yes, I suppose—" he said.

"Eloquence, for one," Queen Elinor continued. "And good luck, of course."

Merida was about to make a face at Young Macintosh . . . until she realized that her mum was keeping an eye on her.

"One might even argue that we've forgotten the emerald's most important meaning—as a symbol of loyalty," Queen Elinor said. "There is an ancient Legend of the Emeralds. And it is part of the reason we are gathered here today."

"For the Rites of Summer?" Merida asked.

Queen Elinor nodded. "Long before the peace that unites our clans, dark days befell our homeland," she began. "There was terrible fighting. The people suffered from the constant battles. Then two great kings— one from each clan—rose to power. They understood that friendship between our clans would be the only way to make peace. So they each brought their clans to the base of the Fire Falls.

"Then the two kings climbed the great falls together. Their people watched in amazement as the kings reached the top of the waterfall. According to legend, the kings each placed an emerald at the source of the Fire Falls—a worthy sacrifice to build

friendship between the clans and prove their loyalty to each other. From that day forth, the Fire Falls' glow at sunset served as a reminder of the two kings' pledge. As long as the Fire Falls run sparkling, we know that there is peace between the clans."

"And there always will be," Lord Macintosh declared.

Just then, King Fergus approached them. "Elinor, these manky lads will eat me alive if the feast doesn't begin with haste!" he said.

"Yes, of course, I'm sure everyone is ready to begin," Queen Elinor said. She and King Fergus stood before the crowd to officially welcome them to the Rites of Summer. But before Queen Elinor could say another word, the heavy wooden doors at the back of the Great Hall crashed open with a loud *bang*.

A DunBroch clansman raced into the hall. Sweat dripped from his red face as he tried to catch his breath. "The Fire Falls—" he gasped. "The Fire Falls—"

"Out with it, man! Say what you've come to say!" King Fergus exclaimed.

"The Fire Falls—they've gone dark!"

CHAPTER FIVE

Everyone in the Great Hall gasped. Then the DunBroch and Macintosh clans started talking all at once, filling the Great Hall with loud voices.

"It cannot be true!" King Fergus shouted above all the noise. "Calm yourselves, people of DunBroch and honored guests from the House of Macintosh. We have come together to celebrate the friendship of our clans.

There is no reason for the Fire Falls to flow with darkness and discord. Come, we shall go see them for ourselves."

King Fergus led the DunBroch and Macintosh clans outside. As everyone headed toward the Fire Falls, Merida uneasily reached for the thistle charm attached to her bow. She hoped that her father was right about the falls . . . but she couldn't forget Queen Elinor's story.

When the clans reached the base of the Fire Falls, it was clear that something was very wrong with the majestic waterfall. Everyone stared up in shock at the dark water that cascaded over the cliff. A black, misty spray coated the rocks that lined the falls. Even the Crone's Tooth was covered in dark water.

King Fergus's face turned red with rage. "Who has done this?" he roared. "Who has threatened the peace between our great clans?"

Lord Macintosh stepped forward and clapped his hand on King Fergus's shoulder. "I stand with King Fergus," he announced. "When he finds out which one of his clansmen caused this, he will have our full support."

King Fergus turned to Lord Macintosh with a frown. "I never said that someone from DunBroch was to blame," he stated.

"Well, it surely wasn't someone from the Macintosh clan," Lord Macintosh replied.

"What makes you so quick to blame the fine people of DunBroch?" King Fergus demanded. "It could just as easily be one of your clansmen."

"Oh, that's a nice display of hospitality!" Lord Macintosh shot back. "Accusing your guests of a crime against our clans."

"My dear lords," Queen Elinor began, trying to calm them before their tempers exploded. But it was too late.

"I'll not have my people insulted by this bilious, blue-faced bandit!" King Fergus howled in outrage.

"And I'll not stay in DunBroch and be insulted!" Lord Macintosh bellowed. "Macintosh clan! Take down the tents and return to the ships. We set sail before nightfall."

"No, you mustn't go!" Queen Elinor exclaimed. "We can still celebrate the Rites of Summer. Our clans are still friends."

"Not anymore," Lord Macintosh snapped. Then he strode away from the Fire Falls.

The DunBroch and Macintosh clans started arguing as they followed Lord Macintosh back to the castle. Soon, only Merida and Young Macintosh were left behind. Merida's mind raced. She held on tightly to the heavy emerald hidden in her pouch.

Merida knew that if she and Young Macintosh had caused all this trouble by taking the emeralds, it would be up to them to set things right. When she looked at the worried expression on Young Macintosh's face, she could tell that he felt the same way.

"We've got to return them," she said to Young Macintosh. "We've got to put the emeralds back. Then our clans can mend their friendship—and celebrate the Rites of Summer as they were meant to do."

Young Macintosh reached into his pouch for the emerald. Even in the bright summer sunshine, it didn't sparkle. The emerald's glow was completely gone.

"Too bad," Young Macintosh said. "I wanted to give this to my father. But I agree that the sooner we return the emeralds, the sooner we can get back to celebrating the Rites of Summer. We'll have to be quick, though. My father will want to set sail as soon as possible."

Merida didn't waste a moment. She tethered Angus, jumped up, and wrapped her hands around one of the strong rocks that lined the Fire Falls. But before she could pull herself up to the next rock, Merida slid back to the ground.

"What kind of jiggery-pokery is this?" Merida said as she tried again. Once more, she slid down the rocks.

"Move aside," Young Macintosh ordered, stepping in front of Merida. He lunged for a higher rock, but he slipped off it just as Merida had.

Suddenly, Merida realized what was

happening. "It's the water!" she exclaimed. "When it splatters on the rocks, it makes them too slippery to climb."

"Not to worry," Young Macintosh said confidently. "We'll take another route to the source. Then we can put the emeralds back and everything will be right."

"But there *isn't* another way to the top of the Fire Falls," Merida said. "At least, none that I know."

A frown flickered on Young Macintosh's face. "If we can't replace the emeralds . . ." he began. Then his voice trailed off. He didn't need to finish his sentence. If they couldn't replace the emeralds and restore the water, war might break out between their clans . . . and everyone would pay for their mistake.

CHAPTER SIX

Merida squinted at the top of the falls, shielding her eyes from the blazing summer sun. There has to be a way to the top of the Fire Falls! she thought.

Suddenly, a cloud passed in front of the sun, casting a shadow over the waterfall. Then Merida saw it: the shimmery blue glow of a will-o'-the-wisp! Merida gasped and grabbed Young Macintosh's arm as another wisp appeared, followed by another, and another.

"There!" Merida exclaimed. She pointed at the wisps that hovered in front of the Fire Falls. "Do you see them?"

"What—what are they?" Young Macintosh asked in astonishment.

"They're will-o'-the-wisps," Merida said, her face shining with hope. "They'll lead us to our destiny!"

"I thought wisps were just in legends," Young Macintosh said.

"No—they're as real as you and I," Merida replied. She watched the wisps flicker, one after another, until they almost reached the top of the falls. Then the cloud drifted away from the sun, and all the wisps disappeared at once.

"Wait!" Merida cried. "Don't go! I don't understand what you want us to do!"

But the wisps were gone.

"*I* know want they want," Young Macintosh announced. "They're telling us to return the emeralds!"

"But we already *know* that," Merida said. "What we *don't* know is how to get to the top of the Fire Falls."

Merida scanned the slippery rocks. All the steely-gray stones looked the same, slick with the dark water from the falls.

"What is that?" Merida asked. She pointed toward the top of the Fire Falls, where the highest wisp had hovered. A small tree with a twisted trunk grew between two rocks.

"That's just a juniper tree," Young Macintosh told Merida. "It must be strong to grow so high."

Merida stared at the juniper tree, deep in thought. "We need another way to climb to the top of the falls," she said thoughtfully. "If only we had a rope or something . . ."

Young Macintosh rummaged around in his pouch. "You mean, like this?" he asked, showing her a long coil of rope.

Merida's eyes lit up as she lunged for the rope. "Yes! Give it here!" she cried.

But Young Macintosh held the rope over Merida's head, just out of her reach. "Why? What do you want with it?" he asked.

"Just give it to me!" Merida exclaimed.

"Not until you tell me why you want it," Young Macintosh retorted.

Merida could tell he wasn't going to budge. "I'll use my strongest arrow to shoot the rope between those two rocks—right by the roots of the tree. Then we can climb up the rope instead of the rocks."

"I have a better idea," Young Macintosh said. "I'll *throw* the rope so that it twists around the branches of the tree."

Merida burst into laughter. "Oh, that's a fine plan," she said sarcastically. "You could never throw the rope that high!"

Young Macintosh narrowed his eyes. "Yes, I could," he said. "Watch me!"

Young Macintosh reached back and threw the rope toward the juniper tree with all his might. But it only made it halfway up the rocks before tumbling back to the ground. Young Macintosh's face turned red with frustration as he threw the rope again and again. But it never reached the tree.

"Fine, then, do it your way!" Young Macintosh finally snapped, tossing the rope toward Merida.

"I will," she shot back.

Merida pulled her strongest arrow out of her quiver. Then she tried to attach the rope to the arrow's shaft. But the rope was so thick that she had trouble tying a firm knot.

"I'll do it," Young Macintosh spoke up.

"I don't need any help!" Merida replied.

"The sailors taught me a new kind of knot on the voyage to DunBroch," Young

Macintosh insisted. "You'll fare better with this knot—I know it."

Merida hated to admit it, but her knots just weren't secure enough. Without saying a word, she handed the rope and the arrow to Young Macintosh.

"Here, I'll show you how to tie it," Young Macintosh offered. "It might come in handy someday."

"All right," Merida said begrudgingly. She watched closely as Young Macintosh looped the rope around the arrow a few times before twisting and tying it into a strong knot.

"There!" Young Macintosh said proudly.

Merida tugged on the rope, but it didn't budge. "That's a fancy knot," she said.

She carefully nocked the arrow against

the bowstring. Merida knew she'd have to shoot so straight and true that the arrow would fly deep into the dirt and wedge itself between the rocks.

As Merida raised her bow, the good-luck charms clicked together. She paused for just a moment to touch the thistle charm. Then Merida pulled back the bowstring, adjusted her aim, and—

Whoosh!

The arrow soared into the sky, trailing the long rope behind it like a tail. Just as Merida had hoped, the arrowhead burrowed into the strip of dirt between the rocks. The arrow's shaft was almost entirely buried! As Young Macintosh started to cheer, Merida exhaled in relief. Then a huge grin spread across her face. Most people wouldn't have been able to make such a difficult shot.

Merida ran over to the rope, which dangled several feet above the ground. She leaped up to grab the rope and gave it a strong tug. The arrow stayed firmly wedged in place.

"Now let's both try," Young Macintosh said as he reached for the rope, too.

Merida held up a hand to stop him. "It will never hold both of us at the same time," she said firmly. "I'll climb up first."

"I'm stronger, so I should go first," Young Macintosh argued.

"That's my best oak arrow; I know it can support me. But you weigh more than I do. What if the arrow broke before you reached the top?" replied Merida. "No, I'll climb up first, and tie the rope to the juniper tree. That will be strong enough for you."

"It's going to be a treacherous climb, with the slick rocks," Young Macintosh said. "Do you really think you're up for it?"

"I know I am," Merida replied.

Young Macintosh looked like he wanted to keep arguing. But he finally stepped aside so that Merida could begin her climb.

"Lasses first, then," Young Macintosh said. "Wait, Merida—"

Merida watched as Young Macintosh opened his pouch and held it out to her. "Want to put your emerald in here?" he asked. "For safekeeping during the climb?"

Merida quickly shook her head. "It's plenty safe in my own pouch," she said.

"But your pouch isn't even closed all the way," Young Macintosh pointed out.

"That doesn't matter," Merida assured him. "The emerald is snug inside."

Merida wrapped her arms around the rope and began to climb. She soon realized that Young Macintosh was right. The rocks were slippery as she stepped on them.

Inch by inch, Merida pulled herself up the rope. Beads of sweat dotted her forehead and her arms were starting to ache, but still she climbed. Merida knew that she wouldn't stop climbing until she reached the top.

The Fire Falls had never seemed so high as they did during that difficult climb. At last, Merida could see the crest.

"Almost there, now," she called to Young Macintosh. Then, with one last tremendous pull, Merida hoisted herself onto the soft green grass that grew beyond the rocks. Her hands stung from the rope.

Merida rested for just a moment before she leaned over the edge of the cliff. She yanked her arrow out of the mountainside and untied the rope. Then Merida looped the rope around the strongest juniper tree branch. She tied it firmly by using the knot Young Macintosh had shown her.

"Young Macintosh!" Merida called as she climbed over the edge. "You can come up now!"

The rope trembled as Young Macintosh started climbing. Merida held her breath. The ground seemed very far away. At last, Merida was relieved to see that Young Macintosh was getting close to the top.

"Oi!" she said. "You're almost there. Just a little bit—"

Snap!

The rope suddenly broke under Young Macintosh's weight. He started to fall!

CHAPTER SEVEN

"Young Macintosh! Grab something!" Merida screamed.

At the last moment, Young Macintosh snagged one of the rocks near the top of the falls. "I'm here," he gasped. "I'm fine."

But as soon as he spoke those words, his fingers started to slide off the rock's slippery surface. "Merida!" Young Macintosh cried. "Please—help—I can't hold on!"

"I'm coming!" Merida cried. She flung herself flat on the ground and reached out as far as she could. Her fingers were just inches from Young Macintosh's hand.

"Grab my hand and I'll pull you up!" Merida called.

Young Macintosh reached for Merida's hand, but she was still too far away. Merida gritted her teeth as she pushed herself as far over the ledge as she dared.

At that moment, Merida's pouch tipped forward, plunging the emerald over the side of the Fire Falls!

"No!" Merida cried.

The emerald teetered on one of the rocks. Merida could reach it. But then she couldn't help Young Macintosh. She had a choice

to make: grab the emerald, or save Young Macintosh.

But it was not really a choice at all. Merida reached out as far as she could and gripped Young Macintosh's wrist. Then she heaved with all her might. Young Macintosh just made it over the edge and safely onto the cliff.

But the emerald tumbled off the ledge. In an instant, it was lost forever in the churning waters of the Fire Falls.

Merida fell back on the grass, breathing heavily. "It's gone," she moaned. "The emerald is gone."

"But you saved my life," Young Macintosh said. "Thank you, Merida. Thank you."

"You're welcome," Merida replied. "But

what are we going to do without the second emerald? How can we fix the Fire Falls now? This is all my fault."

"No, it's *my* fault," Young Macintosh interrupted her. "If my gammy rope hadn't snapped—"

"I should've let you carry both emeralds in your pouch—" Merida argued.

"But *I* never should have taken one of the emeralds to begin with," Young Macintosh said.

"And neither should have I," Merida said quietly.

Young Macintosh opened the flap of his pouch and pulled out the remaining emerald. "What should we do with this?" he asked.

"I don't know." Merida shrugged. She

reached for the emerald. "May I hold it?"

"Sure," Young Macintosh replied.

The emerald was heavy in Merida's hand. She stared into its green depths and remembered the way it had glowed on the stone.

"This is no ordinary gem," Merida finally said.

"I know," Young Macintosh replied in a quiet voice. "I can't explain it, but there's something mysterious about it."

"Yes," Merida said. "But I have a feeling that it belongs in the cave, where we found it. And maybe—maybe this special emerald will be enough to fix the Fire Falls, even without the other one."

Young Macintosh nodded. He put the emerald in his pouch and made sure the flap was closed. Then he held out a hand to help Merida to her feet.

As they walked toward the hidden loch, a new worry began to trouble Merida. If one emerald didn't fix the water, how would she and Young Macintosh get home? The rocks were too slippery to climb without his rope. And no one from their clans knew where they were.

Soon Merida and Young Macintosh

reached the loch. The water was getting worse. It was as dark as a moonless night. Merida started running toward the boulders at the far edge of the loch.

"Come on," she urged Young Macintosh. "Hurry!"

Merida flung aside the tangle of vines that covered the entrance to the cavern. It was darker and colder inside than she remembered. As soon as Merida's eyes adjusted to the dim light, she crept toward the ledge. The golden glow was gone. Merida glanced around the cavern, wondering if there were any wisps about. She would feel much better if a wisp flickered near the platform. It would be a sign that she and Young Macintosh had made the right decision.

But no wisp appeared.

"I have the emerald," Young Macintosh said as he walked up to Merida. "So, should I—"

"Place it on the stone, just as we found it," Merida advised him.

They knelt down at the same time. Then Young Macintosh leaned forward and put the emerald in the exact center of the ledge. Merida crossed her fingers as she waited for the emerald to start glowing. The gem stood there for a moment before it started to wobble back and forth. Then the emerald toppled onto its side and rolled toward the edge of the stone!

Merida lunged for the emerald. She caught it just before it fell off the ledge.

"Och! Clumsy of me," Young Macintosh exclaimed. "You want to put the emerald back?"

"I'll do my best," Merida replied. She ran her hand over the platform, trying to find a small dip that might hold the emerald in place. But it was completely flat and smooth.

Merida frowned in the dim light of the cavern. "The stone is flat, but the emeralds are round," she said. "How on earth did they rest here by themselves?"

"Maybe it really does take two emeralds," Young Macintosh said. He seemed worried. "Maybe the two emeralds supported each other."

"Well, we only have one now," Merida said. "So it will have to stand on its own."

Merida bit her lip as she carefully balanced the emerald in the center of the platform. She held it there for a long moment. Then, when Merida was certain the emerald would stay in place, she slowly moved her hands away.

Once more, the emerald did not glow. When it started to wobble, Merida grabbed it and held it steady. But as soon as she moved her hands, the emerald started to fall again.

"Stay!" she cried. "Just stay—stay in place!"

But the emerald did not stay, and it did not glow.

CHAPTER EIGHT

$\mathcal{M}$erida tried everything she could think of to balance the emerald. But it continued to roll toward the edge of the stone.

"It's not working," Young Macintosh finally said in a flat voice. "We need the other emerald. One is useless without the other."

"No!" Merida exclaimed. "There has to be another way—"

Merida held the emerald safely in her lap. She racked her brain, trying to think of a solution. Out of habit, she reached for her bow. Merida found the thistle charm and started rubbing it. She had never needed luck more than she did right now.

Suddenly, Merida's whole face lit up.

"The legend!" she gasped. "We need to follow the legend!"

Young Macintosh looked confused. "What do you mean?" he asked.

"The two kings," Merida said in a rush. "Each one put an emerald on the stone. I've got to put something there, too!"

Merida's fingers trembled as she carefully removed the thistle charm from her bow. She gently placed it on the stone ledge. Then,

holding her breath, she leaned the emerald against it.

A sparkling flash crackled along the charm like a bolt of lightning. Then, for one brief instant, the emerald started to glow!

"What was that?" asked Young Macintosh, his eyes wide. But the emerald had already turned dark again.

Merida frantically tried to remember everything about the legend. *Two leaders . . . a symbol of loyalty . . . a worthy sacrifice. . . .*

At that moment, everything made sense.

"Quick!" Merida exclaimed. "You've got to put something on the stone ledge, too!"

"Like the two kings in the legend," Young Macintosh realized. In one fast motion, he placed a small knife onto the platform.

Nothing happened.

"No," Merida said. "Not just anything will do. It has to be something that is very special to you—something that really, *truly* matters to you."

Slowly, Young Macintosh nodded his head. "Just like the two kings," he repeated. He sat back on his heels, deep in thought.

Black water continued to bubble under the stone ledge. Merida tried to be patient while Young Macintosh made his decision. She pictured the Macintosh clan loading their ships, instead of staying to celebrate the Rites of Summer. She thought about how the ancient kings had proved their loyalty and sealed their friendship: by placing something of great value in the source of the Fire Falls.

And Merida thought about how much she wanted to climb beside the clear, clean waters of the Fire Falls again.

At last, Young Macintosh made up his mind. He carefully unpinned his family's crest from his kilt sash. Without saying a word, he leaned forward and placed it on the other side of the emerald.

The flash that burst from the emerald was so blinding that Merida and Young Macintosh had to shield their eyes. A halo of green light surrounded the emerald as it lit up with dazzling sparkles. Even Merida's thistle charm and Young Macintosh's crest started to shine!

Then a golden glow flickered under the platform. It spread out until it filled every corner of the cavern with beautiful light.

Crystal-clear water began to pool around the emerald, the charm, and the crest! The light made the water glitter like shooting stars. It flowed over the side of the ledge. When it touched the black water, a spark as green as the emerald shone forth. The black water began to sparkle, too.

"It's working!" Merida cried.

Merida and Young Macintosh ran out of the cavern as more water gushed over the platform. They watched the clear water flow into the murky loch. At first, nothing seemed to happen. Then emerald-green sparks spread across the dark water, transforming it into crystal blue. Merida beamed proudly as she watched the loch shimmer in the sunlight. Soon, she knew, the water would reach the top of the Fire Falls. And Merida wanted to be there when it happened.

"Come on!" she yelled, grabbing Young Macintosh's arm. Together, they ran toward the Fire Falls.

They reached the edge of the cliff just in time to see the clear water cascade over the

Fire Falls. It sparkled like fire as the setting sun reflected off it. The waterfall's spray splashed onto the rocks, washing away all the darkness. Merida knew that she and Young Macintosh would have no trouble climbing down the Fire Falls now. But would they make it back to Castle DunBroch in time to save their clans' friendship?

CHAPTER NINE

Young Macintosh and Merida rode through the meadows toward DunBroch. Merida could hardly wait to share the good news with both clans. But no matter how quickly the horses galloped, the sun seemed to set even faster. Merida remembered Lord Macintosh's announcement that the Macintosh clan would leave by sunset. She hoped that he had changed his mind.

But when Merida and Young Macintosh reached the castle, it was deserted. All the tents had been taken down, and there wasn't a single person to be seen.

"Hurry—to the docks!" Young Macintosh exclaimed. "I hope we're not too late!"

"He wouldn't leave without you," Merida promised him.

Thankfully, the Macintosh ships were bobbing in the water when Merida and Young Macintosh arrived at the dock, Angus rearing to a stop and whinnying. King Fergus and Lord Macintosh stood nearby, still shouting at each other as the Macintosh clansmen finished loading the boats. Then Lord Macintosh noticed his son.

"Young Macintosh!" he yelled. "Get

over here, lad! We set sail at once!"

"Wait!" Merida and Young Macintosh cried together as they dismounted their horses.

Everyone spun around to look at them.

"The Fire Falls are sparkling again!" Merida exclaimed. "The water flows as beautifully as it always has!"

The crowd gasped in surprise. King Fergus, Queen Elinor, and Lord Macintosh quickly pulled Merida and Young Macintosh aside.

"Merida, where have you been?" Queen Elinor asked at once. "And what's this about the Fire Falls? Does the water really run clear again?"

"When everyone left the falls, we stayed behind," Merida explained.

"Merida!" Queen Elinor exclaimed.

"I'm sorry, Mum. It's just—we didn't believe that the water was truly spoiled," Merida replied. "After all, our clans have been friends for a very long time."

"And we always will be," Young Macintosh said firmly.

"Do you mean to say—" Lord Macintosh began. "So you also saw the Fire Falls, lad? With your own eyes?"

"Aye," Young Macintosh said. "The water is back to normal. So we don't have to leave now, do we?"

"After all, there's no reason our clans can't still be friends," Merida added.

King Fergus and Lord Macintosh exchanged a long glance. "Of *course* our clans are the dearest of friends," King Fergus finally said. "It would be a dark day for DunBroch to lose the friendship of the Macintosh clan."

"Aye, but it would be a darker day for us!" replied Lord Macintosh.

"Tonight, we will celebrate," King Fergus announced. "And tomorrow—let the Rites of Summer begin!" Then he glanced at his wife. "It's not too late, is it?" he whispered in her ear.

Queen Elinor consulted the schedule on her scroll. "Scratch the afternoon feast," she mused, "move the welcoming ceremony to the evening feast instead; hold the games in the morning, with dancing and music in the afternoon. No—it's not too late at all!"

Everyone on the dock began to cheer.

Then the DunBroch and Macintosh clansmen began unloading the ships once more.

Merida caught Young Macintosh's eye and smiled. Together, they had saved the Fire Falls . . . and their clans' friendship. And they had even become friends. This year, there was more to celebrate at the Rites of Summer than ever before.